Bliss Carman

Ballads of Lost Haven

A Book of the Sea

Bliss Carman

Ballads of Lost Haven
A Book of the Sea

ISBN/EAN: 9783744766395

Printed in Europe, USA, Canada, Australia, Japan

Cover: Foto ©Andreas Hilbeck / pixelio.de

More available books at **www.hansebooks.com**

Ballads of Lost Haven

A Book of the Sea

By Bliss Carman

Author of Low Tide on Grand Pré, Behind the Arras,
Songs from Vagabondia, &c.

Lamson, Wolffe and Company

Boston, New York and London

MDCCCXCVII

Norwood Press
J. S. Cushing & Co. — Berwick & Smith
Norwood Mass. U.S.A.

Contents

	PAGE
A SON OF THE SEA	7
THE GRAVEDIGGER	8
THE YULE GUEST	12
THE MARRING OF MALYN	26
THE NANCY'S PRIDE	43
ARNOLD, MASTER OF THE SCUD	48
THE SHIPS OF ST. JOHN	55
THE KING OF YS	59
THE KELPIE RIDERS	68
NOONS OF POPPY	93
LEGENDS OF LOST HAVEN	95
THE SHADOW BOATSWAIN	98
THE MASTER OF THE ISLES	104
THE LAST WATCH	110
OUTBOUND	116

A SON OF THE SEA

I was born for deep-sea faring;
I was bred to put to sea;
Stories of my father's daring
Filled me at my mother's knee.

I was sired among the surges;
I was cubbed beside the foam;
All my heart is in its verges,
And the sea wind is my home.

All my boyhood, from far vernal
Bourns of being, came to me
Dream-like, plangent, and eternal
Memories of the plunging sea.

7

THE GRAVEDIGGER

Oh, the shambling sea is a sexton old,
And well his work is done.
With an equal grave for lord and knave,
He buries them every one.

Then hoy and rip, with a rolling hip,
He makes for the nearest shore;
And God, who sent him a thousand ship,
Will send him a thousand more;
But some he'll save for a bleaching grave,
And shoulder them in to shore,—
Shoulder them in, shoulder them in,
Shoulder them in to shore.

8

The Gravedigger

Oh, the ships of Greece and the ships of Tyre
Went out, and where are they?
In the port they made, they are delayed
With the ships of yesterday.

He followed the ships of England far,
As the ships of long ago;
And the ships of France they led him a dance,
But he laid them all arow.

Oh, a loafing, idle lubber to him
Is the sexton of the town;
For sure and swift, with a guiding lift,
He shovels the dead men down.

But though he delves so fierce and grim,
His honest graves are wide,
As well they know who sleep below
The dredge of the deepest tide.

The Gravedigger

Oh, he works with a rollicking stave at lip,
And loud is the chorus skirled;
With the burly rote of his rumbling throat
He batters it down the world.

He learned it once in his father's house,
Where the ballads of eld were sung;
And merry enough is the burden rough,
But no man knows the tongue.

Oh, fair, they say, was his bride to see,
'And wilful she must have been,
That she could bide at his gruesome side
When the first red dawn came in.

And sweet, they say, is her kiss to those
She greets to his border home;
And softer than sleep her hand's first sweep
That beckons, and they come.

The Gravedigger

Oh, crooked is he, but strong enough
To handle the tallest mast;
From the royal barque to the slaver dark,
He buries them all at last.

Then hoy and rip, with a rolling hip,
He makes for the nearest shore;
And God, who sent him a thousand ship,
Will send him a thousand more;
But some he'll save for a bleaching grave,
And shoulder them in to shore, —
Shoulder them in, shoulder them in,
Shoulder them in to shore.

THE YULE GUEST

AND Yanna by the yule log
Sat in the empty hall,
And watched the goblin firelight
Caper upon the wall:

The goblins of the hearthstone,
Who teach the wind to sing,
Who dance the frozen yule away
And usher back the spring;

The goblins of the Northland,
Who teach the gulls to scream,
Who dance the autumn into dust,
The ages into dream.

The Yule Guest

Like the tall corn was Yanna,
Bending and smooth and fair,—
His Yanna of the sea-gray eyes
And harvest-yellow hair.

Child of the low-voiced people
Who dwell among the hills,
She had the lonely calm and poise
Of life that waits and wills.

Only to-night a little
With grave regard she smiled,
Remembering the morn she woke
And ceased to be a child.

Outside, the ghostly rampikes,
Those armies of the moon,
Stood while the ranks of stars drew on
To that more spacious noon,—

The Yule Guest

While over them in silence
Waved on the dusk afar
The gold flags of the Northern light
Streaming with ancient war.

And when below the headland
The riders of the foam
Up from the misty border rode
The wild gray horses home,

And woke the wintry mountains
With thunder on the shore,
Out of the night there came a weird
And cried at Yanna's door.

"O Yanna, Adrianna,
They buried me away
In the blue fathoms of the deep,
Beyond the outer bay.

The Yule Guest

"But in the yule, O Yanna,
Up from the round dim sea
And reeling dungeons of the fog,
I am come back to thee!"

The wind slept in the forest,
The moon was white and high,
Only the shifting snow awoke
To hear the yule guest cry.

"O Yanna, Yanna, Yanna,
Be quick and let me in!
For bitter is the trackless way
And far that I have been!"

Then Yanna by the yule log
Starts from her dream to hear
A voice that bids her brooding heart
Shudder with joy and fear.

The wind is up a moment
And whistles at the eaves,
And in his troubled iron dream
The ocean moans and heaves.

She trembles at the door-lock
That he is come again,
And frees the wooden bolt for one
No barrier could detain.

"O Garvin, bonny Garvin,
So late, so late you come!"
The yule log crumbles down and throws
Strange figures on the gloom;

But in the moonlight pouring
Through the half-open door
Stands the gray guest of yule and casts
No shadow on the floor.

The Yule Guest

The change that is upon him
She knows not in her haste;
About him her strong arms with glad
Impetuous tears are laced.

She's led him to the fireside,
And set the wide oak chair,
And with her warm hands brushed away ,
The sea-rime from his hair.

"O Garvin, I have waited,—
Have watched the red sun sink,
And clouds of sail come flocking in
Over the world's gray brink,

"With stories of encounter
On plank and mast and spar;
But never the brave barque I launched
And waved across the bar.

"How come you so unsignalled,
When I have watched so well?
Where rides the Adrianna
With my name on boat and bell?"

"O Yanna, golden Yanna,
The Adrianna lies
With the sea dredging through her ports,
The white sand through her eyes.

"And strange unearthly creatures
Make marvel of her hull,
Where far below the gulfs of storm
There is eternal lull.

"O Yanna, Adrianna,
This midnight I am here,
Because one night of all my life
At yule tide of the year,

The Yule Guest

"With the stars white in heaven,
And peace upon the sea,
With all my world in your white arms .
You gave yourself to me.

"For that one night, my Yanna,
Within the dying year,
Was it not well to love, and now
Can it be well to fear?"

"O Garvin, there is heartache
In tales that are half told;
But ah, thy cheek is pale to-night,
And thy poor hands are cold!

"Tell me the course, the voyage,
The ports, and the new stars;
Did the long rollers make green surf
On the white reefs and bars?"

"O Yanna, Adrianna,
Though easily I found
The set of those uncharted tides
In seas no line could sound,

"And made without a pilot .
The port without a light,
No log keeps tally of the knots
That I have sailed to-night.

"It fell about mid-April;
The Trades were holding free;
We drove her till the scuppers hissed
And buried in the lee.

*   *   *   *   *   *   *

"O Yanna, Adrianna,
Loose hands and let me go!
The night grows red along the East,
And in the shifting snow

The Yule Guest

"I hear my shipmates calling,
Sent out to search for me
In the pale lands beneath the moon
Along the troubling sea."

"O Garvin, bonny Garvin,
What is the booming sound
Of canvas, and the piping shrill,
As when a ship comes round?"

"It is the shadow boatswain
Piping his hands to bend
The looming sails on giant yards
Aboard the Nomansfriend.

"She sails for Sunken Harbor
And ports of yester year;
The tern are shrilling in the lift,
The low wind-gates are clear.

"O Yanna, Adrianna,
The little while is done.
Thou wilt behold the brightening sea
Freshen before the sun,

"And many a morning redden
The dark hill slopes of pine;
But I must sail hull-down to-night
Below the gray sea-line.

"I shall not hear the snowbirds
Their morning litany,
For when the dawn comes over dale
I must put out to sea."

"O Garvin, bonny Garvin,
To have thee as I will,
I would that never more on earth
The dawn came over hill."

The Yule Guest

*   *   *   *   *   *   *

Then on the snowy pillow,
Her hair about her face,
He laid her in the quiet room,
And wiped away all trace

Of tears from the poor eyelids
That were so sad for him,
And soothed her into sleep at last
As the great stars grew dim.

Tender as April twilight
He sang, and the song grew
Vague as the dreams which roam about
This world of dust and dew:

"O Yanna, Adrianna,
Dear Love, look forth to sea
And all year long until the yule,
Dear Heart, keep watch for me!

"O Yanna, Adrianna,
I hear the calling sea,
And the folk telling tales among '
The hills where I would be.

"O Yanna, Adrianna,
Over the hills of sea
The wind calls and the morning comes,
And I must forth from thee.

"But Yanna, Adrianna,
Keep watch above the sea;
And when the weary time is o'er,
Dear Life, come back to me!"

"O Garvin, bonny Garvin —"
She murmurs in her dream,
And smiles a moment in her sleep
To hear the white gulls scream.

Then with the storm foreboding
Far in the dim gray South,
He kissed her not upon the cheek
Nor on the burning mouth,

But once above the forehead
Before he turned away;
And ere the morning light stole in,
That golden lock was gray.

"O Yanna, Adrianna — "
The wind moans to the sea;
And down the sluices of the dawn
A shadow drifts alee.

THE MARRING OF MALYN

I

THE MERRYMAKERS

AMONG the wintry mountains beside the Northern sea
There is a merrymaking, as old as old can be.

Over the river reaches, over the wastes of snow,
Halting at every doorway, the white drifts come and go.

They scour upon the open, and mass along the wood,
The burliest invaders that ever man withstood.

With swoop and whirl and scurry, these riders of the
    drift

Will mount and wheel and column, and pass into the
  lift.

All night upon the marshes you hear their tread go by,
And all night long the streamers are dancing on the
  sky.

Their light in Malyn's chamber is pale upon the floor,
And Malyn of the mountains is theirs for evermore.

She fancies them a people in saffron and in green,
Dancing for her.   For Malyn is only seventeen.

Out there beyond her window, from frosty deep to deep,
Her heart is dancing with them until she falls asleep.

Then all night long through heaven, with stately to
  and fro,
To music of no measure, the gorgeous dancers go.

The Merrymakers

The stars are great and splendid, beryl and gold and
  blue,
And there are dreams for Malyn that never will come
  true.

Yet for one golden Yule-tide their royal guest is she,
Among the wintry mountains beside the Northern sea.

II

A SAILOR'S WEDDING

THERE is a Norland laddie who sails the round sea-
    rim,
And Malyn of the mountains is all the world to him.
The Master of the Snowflake, bound upward from the
    line,
He smothers her with canvas along the crumbling
    brine.
He crowds her till she buries and shudders from his
    hand,
For in the angry sunset the watch has sighted land;
And he will brook no gainsay who goes to meet his
    bride.

But their will is the wind's will who traffic on the
tide.
Make home, my bonny schooner! The sun goes down
to light
The gusty crimson wind-halls against the wedding
night.

She gathers up the distance, and grows and veers and
swings,
Like any homing swallow with nightfall in her
wings.
The wind's white sources glimmer with shining gusts
of rain;
And in the Ardise country the spring comes back
again.
It is the brooding April, haunted and sad and dear,
When vanished things return not with the returning
year.

A Sailor's Wedding

Only, when evening purples the light in Malyn's dale,
With sound of brooks and robins, by many a hidden
    trail,
With stir of lulling rivers along the forest floor,
The dream-folk of the gloaming come back to Malyn's
    door.
The dusk is long and gracious, and far up in the sky
You hear the chimney-swallows twitter and scurry by.
The hyacinths are lonesome and white in Malyn's
    room;
And out at sea the Snowflake is driving through the
    gloom.
The whitecaps froth and freshen; in squadrons of
    white surge
They thunder on to ruin, and smoke along the verge.
The lift is black above them, the sea is mirk below,
And down the world's wide border they perish as
    they go.

A Sailor's Wedding

They comb and seethe and founder, they mount and
glimmer and flee,
Amid the awful sobbing and quailing of the sea.
They sheet the flying schooner in foam from stem to
stern,
Till every yard of canvas is drenched from clew to
ear'n'.
And where they move uneasy, chill is the light and
pale;
They are the Skipper's daughters, who dance before
the gale.
They revel with the Snowflake, and down the close
of day
Among the boisterous dancers she holds her dancing
way;
And then the dark has kindled the harbor light alee,
With stars and wind and sea-room upon the gurly
sea.

A Sailor's Wedding

The storm gets up to windward to heave and clang
    and brawl;
The dancers of the open begin to moan and call.
A lure is in their dancing, a weird is in their song;
The snow-white Skipper's daughters are stronger than
    the strong.
They love the Norland sailor who dares the rough
    sea play;
Their arms are white and splendid to beckon him away.
They promise him, for kisses a moment at their lips,
To make before the morning the port of missing ships,
Where men put in for shelter, and dreams put forth
    again,
And the great sea-winds follow the journey of the rain.
A bridal with no morrow, no welling of old tears,
For him, and no more tidings of the departed years!
For there of old were fashioned the chambers cool
    and dim,

A Sailor's Wedding

In the eternal silence below the twilight's rim.
The borders of that country are slumberous and wide;
And they are well who marry the fondlers of the tide.
Within their arms immortal, no mortal fear can be;
But Malyn of the mountains is fairer than the sea.
And so the scudding Snowflake flies with the wind
    astern,
And through the boding twilight are blown the shrill-
    ing tern.
The light is on the headland, the harbor gate is wide;
But rolling in with ruin the fog is on the tide.
Fate like a muffled steersman sails with that Norland
    gloom;
The Snowflake in the offing is neck and neck with
    doom.
Ha, ha, my saucy cruiser, crowd up your helm and run!
There'll be a merrymaking to-morrow in the sun.
A cloud of straining canvas, a roar of breaking foam,

A Sailor's Wedding

The Snowflake and the sea-drift are racing in for
    home.
Her heart is dancing shoreward, but silently and pale
The swift relentless phantom is hungering on her trail.
They scour and fly together, until across the roar
He signals for a pilot — and Death puts out from shore.
A moment Malyn's window is gleaming in the lee,
And then — the ghost of wreckage upon the iron sea.

Ah, Malyn, lay your forehead upon your folded arm,
And hear the grim marauder shake out the reefs of
    storm!
Loud laughs the surly Skipper to feel the fog drive in,
Because a blue-eyed sailor shall wed his kith and kin,
And the red dawn discover a rover spent for breath
Among the merrymakers who fondle him to death.
And all the snowy sisters are dancing wild and grand,
For him whose broken beauty shall slacken to their hand.

A Sailor's Wedding

They wanton in their triumph, and skirl at Malyn's
    plight;
Lift up their hands in chorus, and thunder to the
    night.
The gulls are driven inland; but on the dancing tide
The master of the Snowflake is taken to his bride.

And there when daybreak yellows along the far sea-
    plain,   .
The fresh and buoyant morning comes down the wind
    again.
The world is glad of April, the gulls are wild with glee,
And Malyn on the headland alone looks out to sea.
Once more that gray Shipmaster smiles, for the night
    is done,
And all his snow-white daughters are dancing in the sun.

THE LIGHT ON THE MARSH

THE year grows on to harvest, the tawny lilies burn
Along the marsh, and hillward the roads are sweet
    with fern.   ＼
All day the windless heaven pavilions the sea-blue,
Then twilight comes and drenches the sultry dells with
    dew.
The lone white star of evening comes out among the
    hills,   ＼
And in the darkling forest begin the whip-poor-wills.
The fireflies that wander, the hawks that flit and scream,
And all the wilding vagrants of summer dusk and
    dream,

Have all their will, and reck not of any after thing,
Inheriting no sorrow and no foreshadowing.
The wind forgets to whisper, the pines forget to moan,
And Malyn of the mountains is there among her own.
Malyn, whom grief nor wonder can trouble nevermore,
Since that spring night the Snowflake was wrecked
      beside her door,
And strange her cry went seaward once, and her soul
      thereon
With the vast lonely sea-winds, a wanderer, was gone.
But she, that patient beauty which is her body fair,
Endures on earth still lovely, untenanted of care.
The folk down at the harbor pity from day to day;
With a "God save you, Malyn!" they bid her on her
      way.
She smiles, poor feckless Malyn, the knowing smile
      of those
Whom the too sudden vision God sometimes may disclose

Of his wild, lurid world-wreck, has blinded with its
    sheen.
Then, with a fond insistence, pathetic and serene,
They pass among their fellows for lost minds none can
    save,
Bent on their single business, and marvel why men rave.
Now far away a sighing comes from the buried reef,
As though the sea were mourning above an ancient
    grief.
For once the restless Mother of all the weary lands
Went down to him in beauty, with trouble in her hands,
And gave to him forever all memory to keep,
But to her wayward children oblivion and sleep,
That no immortal burden might plague one living thing,
But death should sweetly visit us vagabonds of spring.
And so his heart forever goes inland with the tide,
Searching with many voices among the marshes wide.
Under the quiet starlight, up through the stirring reeds,

The Light on the Marsh

With whispering and lamenting it rises and recedes.
All night the lapsing rivers croon to their shingly bars
The wizardries that mingle the sea-wind and the stars.
And all night long wherever the moving waters gleam,
The little hills hearken, hearken, the great hills hear
and dream.
And Malyn keeps the marshes all the sweet summer
night,
Alone, foot-free, to follow a wandering wisp-light.
For every day at sundown, at the first beacon's gleam,
She calls the gulls her brothers and keeps a tryst with
them.
"O gulls, white gulls, what see you beyond the slop-
ing blue?
And where away's the Snowflake, she's so long over-
due?"
Then, as the gloaming settles, the hilltop stars emerge
And watch that plaintive figure patrol the dark sea verge.

The Light on the Marsh

She follows the marsh fire; her heart laughs and is glad;
She knows that light to seaward is her own sailor lad!
What are these tales they tell her of wreckage on the
shore?
Delay but makes his coming the nearer than before!
Surely her eyes have sighted his schooner in the lift!
But the great tide he homes on sets with an outward
drift.
So will-o'-the-wisp deludes her till dawn, and she
turns home
In unperturbed assurance, "To-morrow he will come."
This is the tale of Malyn, whom sudden grief so
marred.
And still each lovely summer resumes that sweet re-
gard,—
The old unvexed eternal indifference to pain;
The sea sings in the marshes, and June comes back
again.

The Light on the Marsh

All night the lapsing rivers lisp in the long dike grass,
And many memories whisper the sea-winds as they
  pass;
The tides disturb the silence; but not a hindrance
  bars
The wash of time, where founder even the galleon
  stars.
And all night long wherever the moving waters gleam,
The little hills hearken, hearken, the great hills hear
  and dream.

THE NANCY'S PRIDE

On the long slow heave of a lazy sea,
To the flap of an idle sail,
The Nancy's Pride went out on the tide;
And the skipper stood by the rail.

All down, all down by the sleepy town,
With the hollyhocks a-row
In the little poppy gardens,
The sea had her in tow.

They let her slip by the breathing rip,
Where the bell is never still,
And over the sounding harbor bar,
And under the harbor hill.

The Nancy's Pride

She melted into the dreaming noon,
Out of the drowsy land,
In sight of a flag of goldy hair,
To the kiss of a girlish hand.

For the lass who hailed the lad who sailed,
Was — who but his April bride?
And of all the fleet of Grand Latite,
Her pride was the Nancy's Pride.

So the little vessel faded down
With her creaking boom a-swing,
Till a wind from the deep came up with a creep,
And caught her wing and wing.

She made for the lost horizon line,
Where the clouds a-castled lay,
While the boil and seethe of the open sea
Hung on her frothing way.

The Nancy's Pride

.She lifted her hull like a breasting gull
Where the rolling valleys be,
And dipped where the shining porpoises
Put ploughshares through the sea.

A fading sail on the far sea-line,
About the turn of the tide,
As she made for the Banks on her maiden cruise,
Was the last of the Nancy's Pride.

To-day a boy with goldy hair,
In a garden of Grand Latite,
From his mother's knee looks out to sea
For the coming of the fleet.

They all may home on a sleepy tide,
To the flap of the idle sail;
But it's never again the Nancy's Pride
That answers a human hail.

The Nancy's Pride

They all may home on a sleepy tide
To the sag of an idle sheet;
But it's never again the Nancy's Pride
That draws men down the street.

On the Banks to-night a fearsome sight
The fishermen behold,
Keeping the ghost watch in the moon
When the small hours are cold.

When the light wind veers, and the white fog clears,
They see by the after rail
An unknown schooner creeping up
With mildewed spar and sail.

Her crew lean forth by the rotting shrouds,
With the Judgment in their face;
And to their mates' "God save you!"
Have never a word of grace.

The Nancy's Pride

Then into the gray they sheer away,
On the awful polar tide;
And the sailors know they have seen the wraith
Of the missing Nancy's Pride.

ARNOLD, MASTER OF THE SCUD

THERE's a schooner out from Kingsport,
Through the morning's dazzle-gleam,
Snoring down the Bay of Fundy
With a norther on her beam.

How the tough wind springs to wrestle,
When the tide is on the flood!
And between them stands young daring —
Arnold, master of the Scud.

He is only "Martin's youngster,"
To the Minas coasting fleet,
"Twelve year old, and full of Satan
As a nut is full of meat."

Arnold, Master of the Scud

With a wake of froth behind him,
And the gold green waste before,
Just as though the sea this morning
Were his boat pond by the door,

Legs a-straddle, grips the tiller
This young waif of the old sea;
When the wind comes harder, only
Laughs "Hurrah!" and holds her free.

Little wonder, as you watch him
With the dash in his blue eye,
Long ago his father called him
"Arnold, Master," on the sly,

While his mother's heart foreboded
Reckless father makes rash son.
So to-day the schooner carries
Just these two whose will is one.

Arnold, Master of the Scud

Now the wind grows moody, shifting
Point by point into the east.
Wing and wing the Scud is flying
With her scuppers full of yeast.

And the father's older wisdom
On the sea-line has descried,
Like a stealthy cloud-bank making
Up to windward with the tide,

Those tall navies of disaster,
The pale squadrons of the fog,
That maraud this gray world border
Without pilot, chart, or log,

Ranging wanton as marooners
From Minudie to Manan.
"Heave to, and we'll reef, my master!"
Cries he; when no will of man

Arnold, Master of the Scud

Spills the foresail, but a clumsy
Wind-flaw with a hand like stone
Hurls the boom round. In an instant
Arnold, Master, there alone

Sees a crushed corpse shot to seaward,
With the gray doom in its face;
And the climbing foam receives it
To its everlasting place.

What does Arnold, Master, think you?
Whimper like a child for dread?
That's not Arnold. Foulest weather
Strongest sailors ever bred.

And this slip of taut sea-faring
Grows a man who throttles fear.
Let the storm and dark in spite now
Do their worst with valor here!

Arnold, Master of the Scud

Not a reef and not a shiver,
While the wind jeers in her shrouds,
And the flauts of foam and sea-fog
Swarm upon her deck in crowds,

Flies the Scud like a mad racer;
And with iron in his frown,
Holding hard by wrath and dreadnought,
Arnold, Master, rides her down.

Let the taffrail shriek through foam-heads!
Let the licking seas go glut
Elsewhere their old hunger, baffled!
Arnold's making for the Gut.

Cleft sheer down, the sea-wall mountains
Give that one port on the coast;
Made, the Basin lies in sunshine!
Missed, the little Scud is lost!

Arnold, Master of the Scud

Come now, fog-horn, let your warning
Rip the wind to starboard there!
Suddenly that burly-throated
Welcome ploughs the cumbered air.

The young master hauls a little,
Crowds her up and sheets her home,
Heading for the narrow entry
Whence the safety signals come.

Then the wind lulls, and an eddy
Tells of ledges, where away;
Veers the Scud, sheet free, sun breaking,
Through the rifts, and — there's the bay!

Like a bird in from the storm-beat,
As the summer sun goes down,
Slows the schooner to her moorings
By the wharf at Digby town.

All the world next morning wondered.
Largest letters, there it stood,
"Storm in Fundy.   A Boy's Daring.
Arnold, Master of the Scud."

THE SHIPS OF ST. JOHN

Smile, you inland hills and rivers!
Flush, you mountains in the dawn!
But my roving heart is seaward
With the ships of gray St. John.

Fair the land lies, full of August,
Meadow island, shingly bar,
Open barns and breezy twilight,
Peace and the mild evening star.

Gently now this gentlest country
The old habitude takes on,
But my wintry heart is outbound
With the great ships of St. John.

The Ships of St. John

Once in your wide arms you held me,
Till the man-child was a man,
Canada, great nurse and mother
Of the young sea-roving clan.

Always your bright face above me
Through the dreams of boyhood shone;
Now far alien countries call me
With the ships of gray St. John.

Swing, you tides, up out of Fundy!
Blow, you white fogs, in from sea!
I was born to be your fellow;
You were bred to pilot me.

At the touch of your strong fingers,
Doubt, the derelict, is gone;
Sane and glad I clear the headland
With the white ships of St. John.

The Ships of St. John

Loyalists, my fathers, builded
This gray port of the gray sea,
When the duty to ideals
Could not let well-being be.

When the breadth of scarlet bunting
Puts the wreath of maple on,
I must cheer too,—slip my moorings
With the ships of gray St. John.

Peerless-hearted port of heroes,
Be a word to lift the world,
Till the many see the signal
Of the few once more unfurled.

Past the lighthouse, past the nunbuoy,
Past the crimson rising sun,
There are dreams go down the harbor
With the tall ships of St. John.

The Ships of St. John

In the morning I am with them
As they clear the island bar,—
Fade, till speck by speck the midday
Has forgotten where they are.

But I sight a vaster sea-line,
Wider lee-way, longer run,
Whose discoverers return not
With the ships of gray St. John.

THE KING OF YS

WILD across the Breton country,
Fabled centuries ago,
Riding from the black sea border,
Came the squadrons of the snow.

Piping dread at every latch-hole,
Moaning death at every sill,
The white Yule came down in vengeance
Upon Ys, and had its will.

Walled and dreamy stood the city,
Wide and dazzling shone the sea,
When the gods set hand to smother
Ys, the pride of Brittany.

The King of Ys

Morning drenched her towers in purple;
Light of heart were king and fool;
Fair forebode the merrymaking
Of the seven days of Yule.

Laughed the king, "Once more, my mistress,
Time and place and joy are one!"
Bade the balconies with banners
Match the splendor of the sun;

Eyes of urchins shine with silver,
And with gold the pavement ring;
Bade the war-horns sound their bravest
In *The Mistress of the King*.

Mountebanks and ballad-mongers
And all strolling traffickers
Should block up the market corners
With none other name than hers.

The King of Ys

Laughed the fool, "To-day, my Folly,
Thou shalt be the king of Ys!"
O wise fool! How long must wisdom
Under motley hold her peace?

Then the storm came down. The valleys
Wailed and ciphered to the dune
Like huge organ pipes; a midnight
Stalked those gala streets at noon;

And the sea rose, rocked and tilted
Like a beaker in the hand,
Till the moon-hung tide broke tether
And stampeded in for land.

All day long with doom portentous,
Shreds of pennons shrieked and flew
Over Ys; and black fear shuddered
On the hearthstone all night through.

The King of Ys

Fear, which freezes up the marrow
Of the heart, from door to door
Like a plague went through the city,
And filled up the devil's score;

Filled her tally of the craven,
To the sea-wind's dismal note;
While a panic superstition
Took the people by the throat.

As with morning still the sea rose
With vast wreckage on the tide,
And their pasture rills, grown rivers,
Thundered in the mountain side,

"Vengeance, vengeance, gods to vengeance!"
Rose a storm of muttering;
And the human flood came pouring
To the palace of the king.

The King of Ys

"Save, O king, before we perish
In the whirlpools of the sea,
Ys thy city, us thy people!"
Growled the king then, "What would ye?"

But his wolf's eyes talked defiance,
And his bearded mouth meant scorn.
"O our king, the gods are angry;
And no longer to be borne

"Is the shameless face that greets us
From thy windows, at thy side,
Smiling infamy. And therefore
Thou shalt take her up, and ride

"Down with her into the sea's mouth,
And there leave her; else we die,
And thy name goes down to story
A new word for cruelty."

The King of Ys

Ah, but she was fair, this woman!
Warm and flaxen waved her hair;
Her blue Breton eyes made summer
In that bleak December air.

There she stood whose burning beauty
Made the world's high rooftree ring,
A white poppy tall and wind-blown
In the garden of the king.

Her throat shook, but not with terror;
Her eyes swam, but not with fear;
While her two hands caught and clung to
The one man they had found dear.

"Lord and lover," — thus she smiled him
Her last word, — "it shall be so,
Only the sea's arms shall hold me,
When from out thine arms I go."

The King of Ys

Swore he, "By the gods, my mistress,
Thou shalt have queen's burial.
Pearls and amber shall thy tomb be;
Shot with gold and green thy pall.

"And a million-throated chorus
Shall take up thy dirge to-night;
Where thy slumber's starry watch-fires
Shall a thousand years be bright."

Then they brought the coal-black stallion,
Chafing on the bit.   Astride
Sprang the young king; shouted, "Way there!"
Caught the girl up to his side;

And a path through that scared rabble
Rode in pageant to the sea.
And the coal-black mane was mingled
With gold hair against his knee.

The King of Ys

Sure as the wild gulls make seaward,
From the west gate to the beach
Rode these two for whom now freedom
Landward lay beyond their reach.

And the great horse, scenting peril,
Snorted at the flying spume,
Flicked with courage, as how often,
When the tides were racing doom,

Ridden, he had plunged to rescue
From that seething icy hell
Some poor sailor wrecked a-fishing
On the coast. What fears should quell

That high spirit? Knee to shoulder,
King and stallion reared and sprang
Clear above the long white combers
And that turmoil's iron clang.

The King of Ys

What a launching! For a moment,
While the tempest held its breath
And a thousand eyes looked wonder,
Swimming in that trough of death,

Steering seaward through the welter,
Ere they settled out of sight,
Waved above them one gold streamer.
Valor, bid the world good-night! . . .

Not a trace, while the long summers
Warm the heart of Brittany,
Save one stone of Ys, as remnant,
For a white mark in the sea.

THE KELPIE RIDERS

I

Buried alive in calm Rochelle,
Six in a row by a crystal well,

All Summer long on Bareau Fen
Slumber and sleep the Kelpie men;

By the side of each to cheer his ghost,
A flagon of foam with a crumpet of frost.

Hear me, friends, for the years are fleet;
Soon I leave the noise and the street

The Kelpie Riders

For the silent uncompanioned way
Where the inn is cold and the night is gray.

But noon is warm and the world is still
Where the Kelpie riders have their will.

For never a wind dare stir or stray
Over those marshes salt and gray;

No bit of shade as big as your hand
To traverse or trammel the sleeping land,

Save where a dozen poplars fleck
The long gray grass and the well's blue beck.

Yet you mark their leaves are blanched and sear,
Whispering daft at a nameless fear.

While round the bole of one is a rune,
Black in the wash of the bleaching noon.

The Kelpie Riders

"Ride, for the wind is awake and away.
Sleep, for the harvest grain is gray."

No word more. And many a mile,
A ghostly bivouac rank and file,

They sleep to-day on the marshes wide;
Some far night they will wake and ride.

Once they were riders hot with speed,
"Kelpie, Kelpie, gallop at need!"

With hills of the barren sea to roam,
Housing their horses on the foam.

But earth is cool and the hush is long
Beneath the lull of the slumber song

The crickets falter and strive to tell
To the dragon-fly of the crystal well;

The Kelpie Riders

And love is a forgotten jest,
Where the Kelpie riders take their rest,

And blossoming grasses hour by hour
Burn in the bud and freeze in the flower.

But never again shall their roving be
On the shifting hills of the tumbling sea,

With the salt, and the rain, and the glad desire
Strong as the wind and pure as fire.

II

One doomful night in the April tide
With riot of brooks on the mountain side,

The goblin maidens of the hills
Went forth to the revel-call of the rills.

The Kelpie Riders

Many as leaves of the falling year,
To the swing of a ballad wild and clear

They held the plain and the uplands high;
And the merry-dancers held the sky.

The Kelpie riders abroad on the sea
Caught sound of that call of eerie glee,

Over their prairie waste and wan;
And the goblin maidens tolled them on.

The yellow eyes and the raven hair
And the tawny arms blown fresh and bare,

Were more than a mortal might behold
And live with the saints for a crown of gold.

The Kelpie riders were stricken sore;
They wavered, and wheeled, and rode for the shore.

The Kelpie Riders

"Kelpie, Kelpie, treble your stride!
Never again on the sea we ride.

"Kelpie, Kelpie, out of the storm;
On, for the fields of earth are warm!"

Knee to knee they are riding in:
"Brother, brother, — the goblin kin!"

The meadows rocked as they clomb the scaur;
The pines re-echo for evermore

The sound of the host of Kelpie men;
But the windflowers died on Bareau Fen.

Over the marshes all night long
The stars went round to a riding song:

"Kelpie, Kelpie, carry us through!"
And the goblin maidens danced thereto.

73

The Kelpie Riders

Till dawn,—and the revel died with a shout,
For the ocean riders were wearied out.

They looked, and the grass was warm and soft;
The dreamy clouds went over aloft;

A gloom of pines on the weather verge
Had the lulling sound of their own white surge;

A whip-poor-will, far from their din,
Was saying his litanies therein.

Then voices neither loud nor deep:
"Tired, so tired; sleep! ah, sleep!

"The stars are calm, and the earth is warm,
But the sea for an earldom is given to storm.

"Come now, inherit the houses of doom;
Your fields of the sun shall be harried of gloom."

74

The Kelpie Riders

They laid them down; but over long
They rest,—for the goblin maids are strong.

The sun goes round; and Bareau Fen
Is a door of earth on the Kelpie men,—

Buried at dawn, asleep, unslain,
With not a mound on the sunny plain,

Hard by the walls of calm Rochelle,
Row on row by the crystal well.

And never again they are free to ride
Through all the years on the tossing tide,

Barred from the breast of the barren foam,
Where the heart within them is yearning home,—

For one long drench of the surf to quell
The cursing doom of the goblin spell.

Only, when bugling snows alight
To smother the marshes stark and white,

Or a low red moon peers over the rim
Of a winter twilight crisp and dim,

With a sound of drift on the buried lands,
The goblin maidens loose their hands;

A wind comes down from the sheer blue North;
And the Kelpie riders get them forth.

III

Twice have I been on Bareau Fen,
But the son of my son is a man since then.

Once as a lad I used to bear
St. Louis' cross through the chapel square,

The Kelpie Riders

Leading the choristers' surpliced file
Slow up the dusk Cathedral aisle.

I was the boy of all Rochelle
The pure old father trusted well.

But one clear night in the winter's heart,
I wandered out to that place apart.

The shafts of smoke went up to the stars,
Straight as the Northern Streamer spars,

From the town's white roofs, so still it was.
The night in her dream let no word pass,

Nor ever a breath that one could feel;
Only the snow shrieked under my heel.

Yet it seemed when I reached the poplar bole,
The ghost of a voice was crying, "Skoal!

The Kelpie Riders

"Rouse thee and drink, for the well is sweet,
And the crystal snow is good to eat!"

I heeded little, but stooped on my knee,
And ate of a handful dreamily.

'Twas cool to the mouth and slaking at first,
But the lure of it was ill for thirst.

The voice cried, "Soul of the mortal span,
Art thou not of the Kelpie clan?"

"What are you doing there in the ground,
Kelpie rider, and never a sound

"To roam the night but the ghost of a cry?"
Ringing and swift there came reply,

"He is asleep where thou art afraid,
In the tawny arms of a goblin maid!"

The Kelpie Riders

Then I knew the voice was the voice of a girl,
And I marvelled much (while a little swirl ·

Of snow leaped up far off on the plain
Of sparkling dust and died again),

For what do the cloisters know, think ye,
Of women's ways? They be hard to see.

Again the voice cried, "Kin of my kin,
The child of the Sun shall win, shall win!"

'Twas an evil weird that so befell;
Yet I leaned and drank of the bubbling well.

I looked for my face in the crystal spring,
But the face that flickered there was a thing.

To make the nape of your neck grow chill,
And every vein surge back and thrill

The Kelpie Riders

With a passion for something not their own —
In a life their life has never known.

For raven hair and eyes like the sun
Are merry but dour to look upon.

She smiled through her lashes under the wave,
And my soul went forth her bartered slave.

I swore, "By St. Louis, I'll come to thee,
Though I ride to my doom in the gulfs of the sea!

"Thy Kelpie rider shall wake and rue
His ruined life in the loss of you."

Then I fled in the start of a terror of joy,
O'er leagues where a legion might deploy;

For the acres of snow were level and hard,
Every flake like a crystal shard.

The Kelpie Riders

I was the runner of all Rochelle,
Could run with the hounds on Haric Fell;

And something stark as a gust of the sea
Had a grip of the whimsy boy in me.

I ran like the drift on the ice low curled
When the winds of Yule are abroad on the world.

Sudden, the beat of a throbbing sound
Lost in the core of the blue profound:

"Kelpie, Kelpie, Kelpie, come!"
Was it my heart?—But my heart was numb.

"Kelpie, Kelpie!" Was it the sea?
Far on, at the verge of Bareau lea,

I saw like an army, shield and casque,
The breakers roll in the Roads of Basque.

The Kelpie Riders

"Kelpie, Kelpie!" Was it the wolves?
In the dusk of pines where night dissolves

To streamers and stars through the mountain gorge,
I heard the blast of a giant forge.

Then I knew the wind was awake from the North,
And the ocean riders were freed and forth.

Time, there is time (now gallop, my heart!)
Ere the black riders disperse and depart.

The dawn is late, but the dawn comes round,
And Fleetfoot Jean has the wind of a hound.

The hue and cry of the Kelpie horde
Was growing and grim on that white seaboard.

It rolled and gathered and died and grew
Far off to the rear; a smile thereto

The Kelpie Riders

I turned; a fathom behind my ear
A rider rode with a shadowy leer.

I sickened and sped. He laughed aloud,
"Wind for a mourner, snow for a shroud!"

On and on, half blown, half blind,
Shadow and self, and the wind behind!

I slackened, he slackened; I fled, he flew;
In a swirl of snow-drift all night through

I scoured along the gusty fen,
A quarry for hunting Kelpie men.

But only one could hold at my side:
"Brother, brother, I love thy stride.

"Wilt thou follow thy whim to win
My merry maid of the goblin kin?"

The Kelpie Riders

I swerved from my trail, for he haunted my ear
With his moaning jibe and his shadowy leer.

So by good hap as we sped it fell,
I fetched a circuit back for the well.

Like a spilth of spume on the crest of the bore
When the combing tides make in for shore,

That runner ran whose love was a wraith;
But the rider rode with revenge in his teeth.

Another league, and I touch the goal,—
The mystic rune on the poplar bole,—

When the dusky eyes and the raven hair
And the lithe brown arms shall greet me there.

I ran like a harrier on the trace
In the leash of that ghoul, and the wind gave chase.

The Kelpie Riders

A furlong now; I caught the gleam
Of the bubbling well with its tiny stream;

An arrowy burst; I cleared the beck;
And — the Kelpie rider bestrode my neck.

*   *   *   *   *   *   *   *   *

Dawn, the still red winter dawn;
I awoke on the plain; the wind was gone; —

All gracious and good as when God made
The living creatures, and none was afraid.

I stooped to drink of the wholesome spring
Under the poplars whispering:

Face to my face in that water clear —
The Kelpie rider's jabbering leer!

Ah, God! not me: I was never so!
Sainted Louis, who can know

The lords of life from the slaves of death?
What help avail the speeding breath

Of the spirit that knows not self's abode,—
When the soul is lost that knows not God?

I turned me hóme by St. Louis' Hall,
Where the red sun burns on the windows tall.

And I thought the world was strange and wild,
And God with his altar only a child.

IV

Again one year in the prime of June,
I came to the well in the heated noon,

Leaving Rochelle with its red roof tiles
By the Pottery Gate before St. Giles, —
86

The Kelpie Riders

There where the flower market is,
Where every morning up from Duprisse

The flower girls come by the long white lane
That skirts the edge of Bareau plain; —

To the North, the city wall in the sun,
To the left, the fen where the eye may run

And have its will of the blazing blue.
The while I loitered the market through,

Halting a moment to converse
With old Babette who had been my nurse,

There passed through the stalls a woman, bright
With a kirtle of cinnabar and white

Among the kerseys blue; and I said,
"Who is it, Babette, with lifted head,

"And the startled look, possessed and strange,
Under the paint — secure from change?"

"Ah, 'Sieur Jean, do ye not ken
Of the eerie folk of Bareau Fen?"

I blenched, and she knew too well I wist
The fearsome fate of the goblin tryst.

"The street is a cruel home, 'Sieur Jean,
But a weird uncanny drives her on.

"'Tis a bitter tale for Christian folk,
How once she dreamed, and how she woke."

"Ay, ay!" I passed and reached the spring
Where the poplars kept their whispering,

Hid for an hour in the shade,
In the rank marsh grass of a tiny glade.

The Kelpie Riders

There crossed the moor from the town afar,
In kirtle of white and cinnabar,

A wanderer on that plain of tears,
Bowed with a burden not of the years,

As one that goeth sorrowing
For many an unforgotten thing.

To the crystal well as the sun drew low
There came that harridan of woe.

She stooped to drink; I heard her cry:
"Ah, God, how tired out am I!

"I called him by the dearest name
A girl may call; I have my shame.

"'Yet death is crueller than life,'
Once they said, 'for all the strife.'

"And so I lived; but the wild will,
Broken and bitter, drives to ill.

"And now I know, what no one saith,
That love is crueller than death.

"How I did love him! Is love too high,
My God, for such lost folk as I?"

Her tears went down to the grass by the well,
In that passion of grief, and where they fell

Windflowers trembled pale and white.
A craven I crept away from the sight;

And turned me home to St. Louis' Hall,
Where the sunflowers burn by the eastern wall.

The vesper frankincense that day
Rose to the rafters and melted away,

And was no more than a cloud that stirs
Among the spires of Norway firs.

And I said, "The holy solitude
Of the hoary crypt and the wild green wood

"Are one to the God I have never known,
Whose kingdom has neither bourn nor throne."

V

Now I am old, and the years delay;
But I know, I know, there will come a day,—

When April is over the Norland town,
And the loosened brooks from the hills go down,

When tears have quenched the sorrow of time,—
Wherein the earth shall rebuild her prime,

The Kelpie Riders

And the houses of dark be overthrown;
When the goblin maids shall love their own,—

Their arms forever unlaced from their hold
Of the earls of the sea on that alien wold,—

And the feckless light of their golden eyes
Shall forget the desire that made them wise;

When the hands of the foam shall beckon and flee,
And the Kelpie riders ride for the sea;

And the whip-poor-will the whole night long
Repeat his litanies of song,

Till morning whiten the world again,
And the flowers revive on Bareau Fen,

Over the acres of calm Rochelle
Fresh by the stream of the crystal well.

NOONS OF POPPY

Noons of poppy, noons of poppy,
Scarlet leagues along the sea;
Flaxen hair afloat in sunlight,
Love, come down the world to me!

There's a Captain I must ship with,
(Heart, that day be far from now!)
Wears his dark command in silence
With the sea-frost on his brow.

Noons of poppy, noons of poppy,
Purple shadows by the sea;
How should love take thought to wonder
What the destined port may be?

Noons of Poppy

Nay, if love have joy for shipmate
For a night-watch or a year,
Dawn will light o'er Lonely Haven,
Heart to happy heart, as here.

Noons of poppy, noons of poppy,
Scarlet acres by the sea
Burning to the blue above them;
Love, the world is full for me.

LEGENDS OF LOST HAVEN

THERE are legends of Lost Haven,
Come, I know not whence, to me,
When the wind is in the clover,
When the sun is on the sea.

There are rumors in the pine-tops,
There are whispers in the grass;
And the flocking crows at nightfall
Bring home hints of things that pass

Out upon the broad dike yonder,
All day long beneath the sun,
Where the tall ships cloud and settle
Down the sea-curve, one by one.

95

And the crickets in fine chorus —
Every slim and tiny reed —
Strive to chord the broken rhythmus
Of the world, and half succeed.

There are myriad traditions
Treasured by the talking rain;
And with memories the moonlight
Walks the cold and silent plain.

Where the river tells his hill-tales
To the lone complaining bar,
Where the midgets thread their dances
To the yellow twilight star,

Where the blossom bends to hearken
To the bee with velvet bands,
There are chronicles enciphered
Of the yet uncharted lands.

Legends of Lost Haven

All the musical marauders
Of the berry and the bloom
Sing the lure of soul's illusion
Out of darkness, out of doom.

But the sure and great evangel
Comes when half alone I hear,
At the rosy door of silence,
Love, the lord of speech, draw near.

Then for once across the threshold,
Darkling spirit, thou art free,—
As thy hope is every ship makes
Some lost haven of the sea.

THE SHADOW BOATSWAIN

Don't you know the sailing orders?
It is time to put to sea,
And the stranger in the harbor
Sends a boat ashore for me.

With the thunder of her canvas
Coming on the wind again,
I can hear the Shadow Boatswain
Piping to his shadow men.

Is it firelight or morning,
That red flicker on the floor?
Your good-by was braver, sweetheart,
When I sailed away before.

The Shadow Boatswain

Think of this last lovely summer!
Love, what ails the wind to-night?
What's he saying in the chimney
Turns your berry cheek so white?

What a morning! How the sunlight
Sparkles on the outer bay,
Where the brig lies waiting for me
To trip anchor and away!

That's the Doomkeel. You may know her
By her clean run aft; and, then,
Don't you hear the Shadow Boatswain
Piping to his shadow men?

Off the freshening sea to windward,
Is it a white tern I hear
Shrilling in the gusty weather
Where the far sea-line is clear?

The Shadow Boatswain

What a morning for departure!
How your blue eyes melt and shine!
Will you watch us from the headland
Till we sink below the line?

I can see the wind already
Steer the scurf marks of the tide,
As we slip the wake of being
Down the sloping world and wide.

I can feel the vasty mountains
Heave and settle under me,
And the Doomkeel veer and shudder,
Crumbling on the hollow sea.

There's a call, as when a white gull
Cries and beats across the blue;
That must be the Shadow Boatswain
Piping to his shadow crew.

The Shadow Boatswain

There's a boding sound, like winter
When the pines begin to quail;
That must be the gray wind moaning
In the belly of the sail.

I can feel the icy fingers
Creeping in upon my bones;
There must be a berg to windward
Somewhere in these border zones.

Stir the fire. . . . I love the sunlight,—
Always loved my shipmate sun.
How the sunflowers beckon to me
From the dooryard one by one!

How the royal lady roses
Strew this summer world of ours!
There'll be none in Lonely Haven;
It is too far north for flowers.

The Shadow Boatswain

There, sweetheart! And I must leave you.
What should touch my wife with tears?
There's no danger with the Master;
He has sailed the sea for years.

With the sea-wolves on her quarter,
And a white bone in her teeth,
He will steer the shadow cruiser,
Dark before and doom beneath,

Down the last expanse, till morning
Flares above the broken sea,
And the midnight storm is over,
And the Isles are close alee.

So some twilight, when your roses
Are all blown and it is June,
You will turn your blue eyes seaward
Through the white dusk of the moon,

The Shadow Boatswain

Wondering, as that far sea-cry
Comes upon the wind again,
And you hear the Shadow Boatswain
Piping to his shadow men.

THE MASTER OF THE ISLES

THERE is rumor in Dark Harbor,
And the folk are all astir;
For a stranger in the offing
Draws them down to gaze at her,

In the gray of early morning,
Black against the orange streak,
Making in below the ledges,
With no colors at her peak.

Something makes their hearts uneasy
As they watch the long black hull,
For she brings the storm behind her
While before her there is lull.

The Master of the Isles

With no pilot and unspoken,
Where the dancing breakers are,
Presently she veers and races
In across the roaring bar,—

Rounds and luffs and comes to anchor,
While the wharf begins to throng.
Silence falls upon the women,
And misgiving stirs the strong.

Then with some obscure foreboding,
As a gray-haired watcher smiles,
They perceive the fearless captain
Is the Master of the Isles.

They recall the bleak December
Many streaming years ago,
When the stranger had been sighted
Driving shoreward with the snow;

The Master of the Isles

When the Master came among them
With his calm and courtly pride,
And had sailed away at sundown
With pale Dora for his bride;

How again he came one summer
When the herring schools were late,
And had cleared before the morning
With old Alec's son for mate.

There was glamour with the Master;
He had tales of far-off seas;
· But his habit and demeanor
Were of other lands than these.

He had never made the Harbor
But there sailed away with him
Wife or child or friend or lover,
Leaving eyes to strain and swim,—

The Master of the Isles

Strain and wait for their returning;
Yet they never had come back;
For the pale wake of the Master
Is a wandering, fading track.

Just beyond our utmost fathom
Is the anchorage we crave,
But the Master knows the soundings
By the reach of every wave.

Just beyond the last horizon,
Vague upon the weather-gleam,
Loom the Faroff Isles forever,
The tradition of a dream.

There a white and brooding summer
Haunts upon the gray sea-plain,
Where the gray sea-winds are quiet
At the sources of the rain.

The Master of the Isles

There where all world-weary dreamers
Get them forth to their release,
Lie the colonies of the kindred,
In the provinces of peace.

Thither in the stormy sunset
Will the Master sail to-night;
And the village will be silent
When he drops below the light.

Not a soul on all the hillside
But will watch her when she clears,
Dreaming of the Port o' Strangers
In the roadstead of the years.

"Port o' Strangers, Port o' Strangers!"
"Where away?" "On the weather bow."
"Drive her down the closing distance!" . . .
That's to-morrow, but not now.

The Master of the Isles

What imperial adventure
Some wide morning it will be,
Sweeping in to Lonely Haven
From the chartless round of sea!

How imposing a departure,
While this little harbor smiles,
Steering for the outer sea-rim
With the Master of the Isles!

THE LAST WATCH

COMRADES, comrades, have me buried
Like a warrior of the sea,
With a flag across my breast
And my sword upon my knee.

Steering out from vanished headlands
For a harbor on no chart,
With the winter in the rigging,
With the ice-wind in my heart,

Down the bournless slopes of sea-room,
With the long gray wake behind,
I have sailed my cruiser steady
With no pilot but the wind.

The Last Watch

Battling with relentless pirates
From the lower seas of Doom,
I have kept the colors flying
Through the roar of drift and gloom.

Scudding where the shadow foemen
Hang about us grim and stark,
Broken spars and shredded canvas,
We are racing for the dark.

Sped and blown abaft the sunset
Like a shriek the storm has caught;
But the helm is lashed to windward,
And the sails are sheeted taut.

Comrades, comrades, have me buried
Like a warrior of the night.
I can hear the bell-buoy calling
Down below the harbor light.

The Last Watch

Steer in shoreward, loose the signal,
The last watch has been cut short;
Speak me kindly to the islesmen,
When we make the foreign port.

We shall make it ere the morning
Rolls the fog from strait and bluff;
Where the offing crimsons eastward
There is anchorage enough.

How I wander in my dreaming!
Are we northing nearer home,
Or outbound for fresh adventure
On the reeling plains of foam?

North I think it is, my comrades,
Where one heart-beat counts for ten,
Where the loving hand is loyal,
And the women's sons are men;

The Last Watch

Where the red auroras tremble
When the polar night is still,
Lighting home the worn seafarers
To their haven in the hill.

Comrades, comrades, have me buried
Like a warrior of the North.
Lower me the long-boat, stay me
In your arms, and bear me forth;

Lay me in the sheets and row me,
With the tiller in my hand,
Row me in below the beacon
Where my sea-dogs used to land.

Has your captain lost his cunning
After leading you so far?
Row me your last league, my sea-kings;
It is safe within the bar.

The Last Watch

Shoulder me and house me hillward,
Where the field-lark makes his bed,
So the gulls can wheel above me,
All day long when I am dead;

Where the keening wind can find me
With the April rain for guide,
And come crooning her old stories
Of the kingdoms of the tide.

Comrades, comrades, have me buried
Like a warrior of the sun;
I have carried my sealed orders
Till the last command is done.

Kiss me on the cheek for courage,
(There is none to greet me home,)
Then farewell to your old lover
Of the thunder of the foam;

The Last Watch

For the grass is full of slumber
In the twilight world for me,
And my tired hands are slackened
From their toiling on the sea.

OUTBOUND

A LONELY sail in the vast sea-room,
I have put out for the port of gloom.

The voyage is far on the trackless tide,
The watch is long, and the seas are wide.

The headlands blue in the sinking day
Kiss me a hand on the outward way.

The fading gulls, as they dip and veer,
Lift me a voice that is good to hear.

The great winds come, and the heaving sea,
The restless mother, is calling me.

Outbound

The cry of her heart is lone and wild,
Searching the night for her wandered child.

Beautiful, weariless mother of mine,
In the drift of doom I am here, I am thine.

Beyond the fathom of hope or fear,
From bourn to bourn of the dusk I steer,

Swept on in the wake of the stars, in the stream
Of a roving tide, from dream to dream.